Misa Learns to Ride

By Jay Sanders

Illustrated by Pat Reynolds

Bella and Misa were playing
in the yard.

"Come on, Misa," said Bella.
"I want to ride Little Horse.
You can ride, too."

Misa looked scared.

"I don't want to ride Little Horse," she said. "I will fall off."

"No," said Bella.
"You will not fall off.
Little Horse is not very big."

Mom came over to the girls.

Misa looked sad.

"I would like to ride Little Horse," she said,

"but I am scared I will fall off."

Mom smiled at Misa.
"You don't have to ride today.
I will help Bella get Little Horse,
and you can sit under
the big tree."

Mom and Bella got Little Horse
from the paddock.
They put on her saddle and bridle.

Little Horse liked to take Bella
for a ride.

Bella rode Little Horse
up and down the paddock.

Misa smiled, "Bella is a good rider.
I want to be a good rider, too."

Mom smiled at Misa.
"Do you want to pat
Little Horse?" she said.

"Yes, please," said Misa.

Mom and Misa walked over
to Bella and Little Horse.

"Put your hand
on Little Horse's nose," said Bella.
"Then rub your hand up and down."

Misa rubbed Little Horse's nose.
It was warm and soft.

"Do you want to sit
on Little Horse?" said Bella.
"I will be here to help you."

Misa looked at Little Horse.
She had big brown eyes.
She had a warm soft nose.

"Yes," said Misa.
"I will sit on her."

Misa put on Bella's helmet.

Then Mom helped Misa
to get on Little Horse.

Bella smiled at Misa.
"You are very brave.
Do you want to ride
up and down the paddock now?"

"Yes, please," said Misa.

Bella led Little Horse
up and down the paddock.

Mom looked at the girls
and smiled.

"That was good, Misa," she said.

Misa looked very happy.

"Come on," said Bella.
"Let's put Little Horse
back in the paddock.
I want to play on the swing."

"Oh, no!" said Misa.
"I want to ride Little Horse
again and again!"